WITH THIS KISS

Windswept Bay, Book Three

DEBRA
CLOPTON

With This Kiss

CHAPTER ONE

Shar Sinclair stared at her reflection in the mirror and the amazing, but simple, wedding dress that made her look more elegant than she'd ever felt in her life. She was marrying the man of her dreams. And that said a lot considering she'd never actually thought she wanted to marry and share her life with anyone. And then Gage came along.

And suddenly she had her dream man and she was eager to share her life with him.

She stared at herself in the mirror wearing her wedding dress and she tried to calm the turmoil trying to go a little haywire inside her.

Why was she feeling this way? A tremor ran through her, and she breathed in slowly, filling her lungs and holding it a few beats as her stomach tightened into a thousand knots. Twisted, tight knots that threatened to squeeze the cheese crackers she'd eaten for lunch right out of her.

Nothing said non-elegant more than upchucking while wearing her wedding gown.

Shar exhaled heavily and shook herself.

What is wrong with me?

At the rate she was going, she'd have an ulcer before her wedding was over.

"Is Gage here yet?" she asked.

Her older sister, Cali, pushed a shiny strand of her blonde hair behind her ear and smiled with assurance. "Not yet. But I'm sure he'll show up soon."

Shar moistened her dry lips.

Instantly Jillian was at her side with a tube of gloss. She and Jillian were two of a trio of triplets and though they didn't look alike, they did share a keen sense about how the others were feeling, which Jillian

With This Kiss

A kiss is just a kiss…or so some say. But I disagree…this kiss can change a life. It did mine.

You are officially invited to the wedding of Shar Sinclair to the man of her dreams, Gage Lancaster…if the groom ever makes it to the wedding.

Where is Gage?

There's only an hour until the ceremony—no one has heard from Gage and he's not answering his phone. Now, Shar's ready to go looking for her man because something just doesn't feel right.

After receiving the message he's been waiting for from his private investigator, Gage can't help but make a life-changing stop on his way to his wedding.

But, things quickly spiral out of control and everything about this wedding day is about to change…

acknowledged in the look she gave her and her words. "Stop being a nervous wreck. And here, at the rate you're licking those lips, they'll be chapped before Gage gets to kiss you in the ceremony."

Cali smiled into the mirror. "True, and that isn't the fun way to get them chapped."

Shar laughed despite her nerves and let Jillian run the rosy gloss over her lips. She was not used to having this much makeup on or her sisters hovering so much. But it was sweet and she was grateful right now to have them beside her.

"I've never worn so much makeup or lip gloss in all my life," she reminded them. "Gage may not recognize me when he finally gets here."

Jillian rolled her eyes. "He'll recognize you."

Tears suddenly pricked at her eyes. And a wave of panic rolled through her.

Where are you, Gage? Three months ago, she was afraid of losing her independence and today she couldn't get his ring on her finger fast enough. If only her man would make it to the church on time, they'd get this ceremony out of the way and start their lives together.

She looked at the clock…one hour to go and he was not here with his groomsmen, getting into his tux. No matter what Jillian and Cali said, it wasn't right. He'd told her he couldn't wait to be her husband. That he'd be there ready and waiting to put a ring on her finger and to kiss her breathless. But he wasn't here. And she could deny it all she wanted but the truth was that her groom was missing.

"Relax, Shar. He'll be here." Cali gently rubbed Shar's back and their gazes met in the mirror once more. "He will be here." Cali enunciated each word carefully.

Always the encourager, her older sister was trying hard to do just that.

"He said he would be here early. It's now inside of an hour and he's missing."

Cali's expression tensed. "He's not missing. He's just running late or something."

Not a patient person, Shar gritted her teeth. Patience had never been her strong point; if she wanted something, she went out and got it or acted. She was strong-willed that way and it worked for her. Waiting did not. "Jillian, please poke your head out the door again. Just to make sure he's not out there. Something isn't right. I feel it and there is no denying it."

Both her sisters stared at her and knew she'd reached her limit.

"It's just cold feet," Cali said, still trying one last time.

Jillian's brow knitted. "No, I can't imagine it being cold feet. Cali, you were on your extended honeymoon when Shar was moping around for weeks after Gage had left the island. She was climbing the walls when she didn't think he was coming back. This is not cold feet."

Shar sent Jillian a grateful look for finally acknowledging that she wasn't overreacting. "Nope, no cold feet here. I love him. More than I ever dreamed was possible. I mean, because of my love for him I look at my life that I was so protective of, and now am thrilled to get to share it with him. Not hoard it away just for me." She felt weak-kneed suddenly and she couldn't breathe. "It's…where is he?" She gasped as tears surged up and threatened to overcome her. "I need to get this dress off and go find him." She grabbed for her zipper.

"Wait!" her sisters exclaimed together.

Jillian rushed forward and put her hands on Shar's. "Just wait, Shar. You can't take your dress off. People will be arriving soon. He will be here. He's still got over forty-five minutes."

Shar glared at her triplet. "You're right." She shook her head, hoping to clear the panic from it. "This is so not like me."

Cali wrapped an arm around her waist and gave her a one-armed hug. "Come on, little sister. It's time for you to sit down. If Olivia were here, she'd tell you to chill out."

Olivia. Once again, her other triplet hadn't made it to one of their weddings. Shar had been worrying about her lately, too. She wasn't calling much and though she said she was coming, there was always an excuse at the last minute. Olivia had missed Cali's wedding and now hers.

"I wish Olivia had made it. I'm worried about her. This isn't like her either."

Cali handed her a glass of water. "Shar, you cannot fix everyone. Yes, you are Superwoman in my eyes with the way you rescue sea turtles and watch over the injured ones at the Sea Turtle Hospital. But, you worry too much for a straight shooter like you. Olivia is fine. When she's ready to come back home, she will. Right now she's busy keeping the Hollywood elite out of hot water. She'll come home when she can. Until then, we just need to let her live her life."

"True," Jillian agreed. "This is about you, anyway, and you're adding stress to your beautiful day that doesn't need to be here."

Shar's heart thundered and her stomach had coiled into a thousand knots now. "You're right. I just wish he'd found Brandon. He'd hoped that in the two months since we set this wedding date that the private investigator would have good news about his missing brother. But the promising lead he thought he had hasn't come through."

"I can't imagine how Gage must feel. Just learning he has a brother at the reading of his father's will." Cali glanced at Jillian, and Shar saw them struggling to be a unified front for her.

She rubbed her forehead. "I can understand him wanting to find Brandon and to have him at the wedding. We can't imagine having no family at all—we have such a huge one. But when you've just had your dad and then lost him…it's different. Surely…" Her words trailed off as she left her thoughts unspoken…*surely he hadn't decided not to show because his lost brother hadn't been found yet.*

"Maybe something will turn up while you two are on your honeymoon," Cali encouraged once more.

"Yes, maybe it will." Jillian looked hopeful as she headed toward the door. "I'm going to go walk to the parking lot and see if any of the guys have heard anything."

"Thank you," Shar said in a rush, pushing away any thoughts about Gage not showing on purpose. *He would be here.* "And let me know the minute you know."

Jillian shot her that calming, sweet smile of hers. "Well of course." She laughed gently. "Take deep breaths and relax. I'm on this."

That was just it; Shar needed to be on it. She was, after all, a control freak and she knew it. When the door closed behind her, she heaved a heavy sigh. "And so we wait."

"Yes." Cali sat on the chair beside her. "And don't think I'm not watching you and know what's running through your head. Don't even think about going to the bathroom and climbing out the window to go hunt for him."

Shar laughed…because that was exactly the thought that had just crossed her mind and she'd been thinking she would do.

He shouldn't stop.

But he couldn't pass it up and so Gage found himself pulling into the boat docks just as a police car flew past him, headed down the road with his siren blaring.

The moment Gage heard the siren, he'd thought of the Sea Turtle Hospital's rescue ambulance, the one that usually meant Shar was near. But it had a distinctive siren that he could recognize instantly and so he'd known it wasn't the turtle ambulance.

As he parked his car and got out, another police car raced down the road past the entrance of the boating dock. He paused to watch it turn down a side road.

Something was going on and he wondered whether Levi, Shar's brother and chief of police, would be involved. He hoped not because the wedding was happening within the hour and Shar would want Levi and all of her brothers at the wedding. She'd want him there more, so why was he stopping here?

He pulled his phone out and looked at the address on the text message he'd just received. He hoped Shar wasn't having a nervous breakdown or about to come looking for him. He should be there and he would make it on time.

He just needed to see whether his brother was on this boat.

He expected his phone to ring any minute and he hated that he was running late. But, he'd gotten the email and then the address texted to him from the private investigator only moments ago. He'd been headed to the Windswept Bay Resort, where the wedding would be held, but the news he'd been waiting for had finally come.

His brother was indeed living in Windswept Bay.

They'd been searching for Brandon Jackson; the

message said that his name was now BJ McCall. That he'd been adopted by his stepfather around a year after his mother had disappeared with him.

The message said that he was supposed to be on his boat at this dock.

Gage was thirty-one and his brother was about four years younger than him and had been missing since he was about three, so today would be ending about a twenty-four-year-long search.

What would Brandon think about having a brother?

Gage looked at his watch again. He had an hour to get to the resort so he could marry the woman of his dreams, so he better get this show on the road.

He stepped onto the dock and headed down the planked runway between the rows and rows of sailboats and deep-sea fishing boats. It was a quiet day. Seagulls drifted overhead like lazy kites, dipping and soaring and watching for fish in the water. Many of the boat slips were empty as, with most gorgeous days, fishing was a priority of the bay area. Or just heading out to enjoy the blue waters of Windswept Bay. He stopped when he reached the *Morning Glory*, the name of the boat listed in the email and the text.

It was a nice-sized deep-sea fishing boat. But the fact that it was nearly five o'clock in the afternoon and most of the charter boats were out with paying clients and this one sat in its slip made him wonder why. The sound of the mutterings coming from the cabin had him pausing before he stepped onto the deck. With little time to spare, he boarded the boat.

He had a wedding to get to.

Standing Shar up was not an option. It would hurt her too deeply.

"Anyone on board?" he called.

There was no answer. But Gage had heard the mutterings, so he knew someone was inside the cabin. "I just want to ask you a couple of questions," he called louder. There was no way he was walking away before possibly meeting his brother.

He heard murmurs of what sounded like two voices. He waited and then a man with lighter hair than Gage's came up out of the hull. He had a little grease on his hands and he was looking down as he wiped them on a rag. Gage tried to find a resemblance to himself in the tanned skin and the squared jaw. But there wasn't any.

"What questions?" The man lifted his gaze and pinned Gage with icy, teal-blue eyes.

Gage's adrenaline kicked up as he looked into the exact same eyes as his. And also the same eyes as his father's, Milton Lancaster. It was an undeniable genetic gift that he'd evidently passed down to both of his sons.

The impact that he was staring at his brother was almost overwhelming.

It felt as if the boat were hit by a tidal wave as the reality set in and the world rocked around Gage.

"What can I do for you?" Brandon—or BJ—asked, briskly. His gaze took in Gage's tux and then shifted back toward the opening to the cabin. "I'm thinking you're not dressed for an outing today. And I hate to break it to you, buddy, but if you just got married, your new bride is not going to want to go out on a fishing charter at this moment."

"Actually, I'm on my way to get married." Gage thought of Shar. "And you might be wrong about her not wanting to be on the water, at least." He held out his hand. "I'm Gage Lancaster, by the way."

Gage watched the other man's expression for any signs of recognition. He saw none. Nothing, not even a flicker of anything, that hinted that Brandon knew who he was. But Gage *knew* this was his brother. If there had been any doubts about it not being Brandon, the eyes proved it to Gage one hundred percent.

His brother stared hard at Gage's outstretched hand and then he looked down at his grease-streaked hands. "I don't think your bride will appreciate you getting grease on your wedding fingers. Maybe you should leave and come back after the honeymoon." He hitched a brow and his eyes narrowed. Then he yanked his head toward the dock. "It's a good time to leave."

So his brother wasn't the most sociable guy. One of the first business rules Gage had learned from his dad, when he was not much older than ten, was to never take no for an answer. "I actually came to ask a few questions."

His brother's jaw tensed and his gaze shifted toward the cabin.

Gage followed the movement and thought he saw a

shadow flicker in the opening. Something didn't feel right. *Was there someone just inside the cabin doorway?* "Is there a problem?"

BJ's blue eyes chilled. "*No.* Look, I need to get back to work on my motor." His eyes had narrowed as they shifted once again back to the cabin. "And you look like you need to get to a wedding."

Gage should leave. He should turn around and walk off that boat and get the dickens to the resort and marry Shar. But this was his brother and something did not feel right.

And Gage had always had good instincts. So instead of heading off the boat, he took a step toward the cabin. "I'm running late, but I've got time. I need to ask you a few questions."

BJ took a step toward the cabin to block his path. "You don't want to ask me any questions. Go on. Get off my boat," he snapped.

"Too late," a man growled and stepped from where he'd been hidden just inside the cabin. He held a gun in one hand and he pointed it straight at Gage. "If the man wants to ask questions, he can do it while you're driving this boat down the coast."

Gage's stomach clenched and he thought of Shar standing alone, waiting for him.

What had he done?

CHAPTER TWO

Jillian tried not to let her imagination run away with her as she hurried to find her brothers. Shar was not the nervous type and Jillian had never seen her so tied up in knots. She said a prayer that Gage would be with her brothers when she found them.

She rushed through the resort's courtyard, past the kids and families playing in the pool area, and then she turned down one of the landscaped paths that she'd created at the resort and rounded the corner to where the parking area was. They'd designated this area for the wedding party to park. She scanned the cars. Gage's was not in the lot.

Her stomach rocked. *Where was Gage?* There was now only thirty minutes until the ceremony and Gracie, the resort manager and acting wedding planner, had told her that the wedding guests were arriving. Jillian's mouth was dry as she swallowed the lump that had formed in her throat and headed to the private suite the guys were using as their dressing room.

Levi had his phone to his ear and paced outside the room. Her brothers, Cam, who'd driven in from his ranch in Texas, and Max stood with Cali's husband Grant. The three were in deep discussion and did not look happy.

So they were all worried too.

Her other two brothers, Jake and Trent, were coming up the path from the direction of the beach where the wedding would be held and there was worry on their faces too.

"He's nowhere to be found," Jake said, exasperation ringing in his voice as he met up with the others.

Trent rubbed the back of his neck. "This isn't good."

Jillian took a deep breath and stopped beside them. “Where could he be? Shar is literally about to jump in her Jeep and go searching for him. Cali is doing her best to calm her. But we can both read her and you know Shar—she doesn’t sit well. If he doesn’t get here soon, she’ll go find him.”

Cam yanked his Stetson off. The official Sinclair cowboy in the family, Cam looked as if he might be ready to lead a posse out to find Gage. Maybe string him up and then ask questions.

“What’s this guy’s problem?” he snapped. “He sounds like he led her on for two months and now he’s making her wait. I’m not liking this.”

“He didn’t lead her on,” Jillian assured him. “So step back, cowboy. If he doesn’t get here then that means something is wrong. Gage would not stand her up.”

“I’ve got to agree with Jillian,” Jake offered, looking serious. “He’d be here.”

Her other brothers agreed.

Cam let out an exasperated breath. Like Shar, he had little patience. “Okay, so does *anyone* have any idea where he might be?"

Levi hung up his phone and joined the group. There were storm clouds in his eyes. "Well, I don't know if he's there, but a convenience store on the corner of Sand Dollar and Avenue A was robbed about thirty minutes ago and the clerk was shot. My deputies have roadblocks up and are actively searching for the shooter. He was on foot, they believe. There is a possibility that Gage got caught up in the roadblock and is trying to get here but is running behind."

"Man, this is getting better and better," Max said, with dry sarcasm.

Jillian placed her hand on her churning stomach. "But, he's not answering his phone. Why isn't he answering his phone?"

Levi met her gaze. "That's got me puzzled too."

Jillian frowned. "You mean worried." She hated when her brothers, most specifically her older brothers Cam and Levi, thought she couldn't handle knowing things. She guessed it was just brotherly protectiveness but at this moment she didn't have patience for it. "Do you think he could be in trouble?"

Levi cocked his head and gave her that don't-make-me-tell-you-straight look. "Don't go jumping to conclusions. He's still got"—he checked his watch—"a little time."

Jillian let out a loud grunt. "Y'all should all be lined up and ready for Shar. The guests are probably wondering what's going on. Shar may have already locked Cali in a closet and taken off with her wedding dress flapping in the breeze." Jillian had never felt so helpless. She stared at all of her brothers.

Levi's phone rang. He put it to his ear. "What you got?"

Everyone watched him. He hung up. "I've got to go. There's reports of gunshots at the boat dock. I need to be there." He started to loosen his tie. "Go try to keep Shar calm. And call me if Gage shows up."

"I'm coming with you," Cam said.

"No," Levi said firmly. "You have to stay. If Gage does show up, then this wedding can go on without me. But not without all of you. Shar is going to need you all here. I'll keep you posted."

He didn't wait for more protest but headed toward

the parking lot.

Jillian rubbed her temple and groaned. "This day is falling apart. Someone needs to break it to the guests that we may have a delay."

"I'll do it," Cam drawled. "We better all head that way. If he does show up, he'll come straight there."

Jillian was already walking down the path. She felt almost desperate to get to Shar.

She just hoped Shar was still on the property.

Shar was in love. Madly, deeply undeniably in love.

The time since she and Gage had declared their love for each other had been one of complete and total bliss.

Okay, so she was stretching things just a wee bit. He had flown back and forth between Windswept Bay and Manhattan each week, taking care of the company he and his father had built. And he'd been almost obsessed with finding the brother he'd just learned he had at the reading of his dad's will.

He'd wanted to find him before the wedding and there had been hope that it could happen because the private investigator who had been hunting for him all these years had come up with a lead right before Gage's dad had died.

Learning that he had a brother who'd been missing since Gage was a child had been a blow to Gage. It was understandable that he would want to find his brother.

But because of that, Gage hadn't been around as much as Shar had hoped. Yes, he'd come back to Windswept Bay to win her heart but, he had so much on his plate she was now wondering whether he might have started having second thoughts.

She stared at the clock. *Five minutes till six.* The guests were waiting and she was too. And he was not here.

"He isn't out there, is he?" Shar demanded.

Cali had been speaking to Gracie at the door. She turned back and her expression said it all. "He's not."

The door opened and Jillian came inside, along with her mother. Both of them looked pale.

"What's wrong?" Shar rushed forward.

"Well," Jillian squeaked. "He's not here and Cam thought it best to warn the guests that things were behind schedule."

Shar's mother came forward. Violet Sinclair was a beautiful woman, with a huge, loving heart. "I feel sick about this, honey." She took Shar's hands and studied her sympathetically. "But he will show up."

Shar felt ill. "Does anyone know anything that I don't know? Shoot straight. I mean it."

"Okay." Jillian sighed. "Here is the deal. Levi got word that there was a holdup and the clerk was shot. The robber is on foot and they are searching for him. There are roadblocks and he thinks there's a possibility that Gage is caught up in that."

Shar's heart thundered. "He's not answering his phone."

"I know—I said the same thing. And, well, Levi just left. There was a report that gunshots were heard at the boat dock. So he had to go."

"It just doesn't make sense." Shar paced. "If Gage could call me, he would. He would answer his phone."

"Maybe his phone is dead." Cali looked from her mom to Shar. "Jumping to conclusions is not helping this situation."

“Cali is right,” Violet said, calmly.

“Stop. Just stop,” Shar said. “I love all of you, but don’t stand there and tell me to calm down. This isn’t right. Nothing about it feels right.” She yanked her wedding veil out of the bun in her dark hair.

“No,” Cali and her mother exclaimed at the same time and rushed forward.

Shar pushed it into Cali’s outstretched hands. “Hold that. And either someone unzips this dress or I’ll either rip it off or wear it to go look for Gage.”

The moment Gage saw the gun, it went off. A warning shot fired into the dock behind.

The thug snarled to BJ, “You’ll get me out of here or the next bullet takes wedding boy out. And messes up his fancy tux.”

Gage’s heart pounded and everything seemed to go into slow motion as he pulled his focus off the gun and looked at his brother. His mind whirled through possibilities of what his next move should be. Boardrooms and negotiations had been his life, and now his mind reacted, searching as BJ slammed him with a glare.

"I tried to get you to leave. What's wrong with you, man? You've got a bride waiting on you and you're here to ask me questions? There are no questions that important. Not for a fishing boat."

The gun swung toward BJ and the gunman growled, "Move it. Now. I don't have time to stand around here while you two argue. Especially now that I've fired my gun."

BJ stiffened. "You keep waving that thing around like that and I'm going to get mad." There was a steel edge to his voice. "Waving it at me is one thing. But now, you're threatening my guest."

The gunman let out a string of curses and stepped farther into the sunlight. "Just drive the boat or I *will* shoot the groom and toss him overboard for fish food."

BJ slid his icy-blue gaze to Gage and then back to the gunman. "Well, you see, there's a problem. If it was just me, I could have done as you asked as soon as I got my spark plug changed. But now, I feel obligated to get the groom to the church on time."

Gage decided in that moment that his brother was either drunk or not the smartest cookie on the block. Or cut from the same cloth as their dad, a man who'd never backed down from a fight—his fights had just been done in the boardroom.

Or he was bluffing—that, too, was a trait of their dad's. Gage knew how to bluff. Knew how to play his hand in the boardroom like the best poker players Vegas had to offer. But he wanted to make it out of this situation alive. He wanted to marry Shar and start their future together. He wanted to tell BJ he was his brother. They needed to bide their time, not push buttons.

"I'm already late for the wedding. What are you hiding from?" he asked the gunman.

Sweat beaded on the man's forehead. "None of your business." He stepped forward and pointed the gun at BJ. "I'm giving you one more warning. Move."

"Why are you doing this?" Gage asked.

"It's none of your business. All you two need to know is that I need this boat moving. And I need it moving now."

"Like I said, no can do, buddy. Gage has a bride waiting on him."

There was a warning in BJ's eyes and Gage caught it. This was not going to go well. His instincts were telling him to play along with the gunman and make it out of the situation alive.

But as he saw the gunman's finger twitch, his gut told him now was the time to act.

Shar's beautiful ferocious expression flashed before him. The expression she wore when she was fighting to save a sea turtle's life. He had to get to the beach.

When the gunman glared at BJ, taking the bait his brother was tossing at him, Gage reacted, deciding this was his best shot. He kicked upward hard; his foot hit the gunman's wrist and then Gage charged.

BJ reacted too. They both rammed the assailant together, slamming him up against the boat cabin. Gage grabbed for the gun hand just as the gun fired.

Shar had just grabbed for the zipper of her wedding dress when the door opened and Cam and her dad rushed into the room.

Sam Sinclair's serious gaze found Shar. "Sharleen, honey—"

Cam looked impatiently from their dad back at her.

"What's happened?" Her fingers shook on the zipper and let go.

Cam strode across the room and took her arm. "You need to come with me."

Her knees nearly buckled but Cam's hand tightened on her arms to steady her. "Hang in there, sis."

"What's going on?"

"The robber of the convenience store robbery took two hostages at the boat dock and one has been shot. Levi called. It's Gage."

Like melting butter, Shar wilted, but her dad wrapped his arm around her waist; he and Cam gave her support.

"He's alive, honey," her dad said, sounding as if he were calling to her from a long way off.

"He's alive," Cam repeated. "We need to get you there."

Shar was already moving. *She needed to get to Gage.*

CHAPTER THREE

All of her brothers were waiting in the hallway as Shar rushed from the resort suite with Cam and her dad. A wave of love flowed through her at the concern for her and their show of support as they all fell into line behind her with her sisters and her mother. Strength surged from the shocked depths of her soul and filled her.

She blinked back tears as she clutched the skirt of her wedding dress into her fists and got it out of her way as she hurried to the double doors that Jake held open for her. Once in the courtyard, she ran.

"Where's your car?" She looked over at Cam, who was running with her.

He took the lead. "Follow me. We're supposed to

meet the ambulance at the hospital."

People stopped what they were doing and watched as the entire wedding entourage raced through the resort and to the parking lot. Cam raced to the driver's side of his truck and her dad, who'd been right with them, yanked open the passenger door and helped her hop in. He hopped into the backseat and Cam tore out of the parking lot instantly.

"Buckle up," Cam demanded, glancing her way and then refocusing on the road ahead.

She grabbed the seat belt and pulled it tight as he flew out onto the main drag and burned rubber as the truck fishtailed into traffic. She didn't have to tell him to hurry.

"How bad is he?" she managed, barely noticing the way they were weaving through traffic.

"Levi just said I need to get you there as fast as possible. That's all I know. So hang on tight."

She did and prayed Gage was doing the same.

BJ paced outside the hospital and let the events on his boat replay in his mind.

He had felt the groom slump to the ground the instant the gunshot sounded. He'd struggled with the shooter and managed to knock the gun from his hand and then he'd gotten him with a strong uppercut and knocked his lights out. Immediately BJ had rushed back to the groom; he was slumped over and blood pooled around him.

BJ didn't have time to feel anything as he turned the man over. He was bleeding from his side. BJ spotted the rag he'd dropped earlier and grabbed it and pressed it to the wound.

"Hold on, man. I hear cops near. Help is on the way."

Gage's eyes opened, blue eyes that looked somehow familiar to BJ. "Shar," Gage grunted. "Tell her…I love her."

"You tell her yourself, bud. I'm telling you, hold on."

That had happened moments before police had swarmed his boat. The first man who moved on board wore a tux too. Same color as the groom's.

He took charge directing his men as he dropped to

his knee. "Gage," he said as the uniformed cops quickly carted off the thug and paramedics moved in to take over caring for Gage.

BJ moved back and let them in. The tuxedo-wearing head cop looked gravely concerned and it didn't take a large IQ to figure out there was a connection.

"Gage, come on—open your eyes," the cop said, his voice gruff. "You hang in there or my sister will personally kill me. Gage," he snapped when there was no response. The paramedics were taking his blood pressure as one had taken over applying pressure. The cop didn't let go of his hand. "I said hang in there, Gage. You have a wedding to get to, so suck it up and hold on."

Gage opened one eye and BJ could have sworn the man's lip twitched, hooking into a slight smile on one side. "I hear." He worked hard but finally managed the last word. "You."

BJ found a smile, too, as he watched the groom and knew he was thinking about his bride, who sounded like a fireball.

"I've got to let the paramedics take care of you. I'm here, though, and Shar will be at the hospital. She's on her way."

BJ hadn't been the one to bring the guy onto his boat and he'd done everything he could to get the man to leave but he'd persisted. BJ had been rude—downright hostile—and still the man had remained. And blast it all, he was certain that Gage had realized danger was on the other side of that cabin door and yet he'd stepped toward it rather than retreat like BJ had tried to make him do. Even knowing he'd done everything he could to warn off the groom, BJ felt guilt weigh over him like a mudslide.

The tux-clad cop had stood then, and his brows were etched together over penetrating eyes as he studied BJ. "Come with me. I have questions."

They moved out onto the dock so the emergency team could extract the groom and get him to the hospital.

"First, who are you and what happened? Why was he on your boat when he should have been at his wedding?"

"BJ McCall." BJ rammed a hand through his hair. "And I have no idea why he was on my boat."

"What happened with the gunman? Why was he on your boat and what connection do you have to him?"

"No connection. I was working on an engine problem, changing out spark plugs and trying to figure out why it was behaving badly when the thug rushed into the cabin, waving his gun around and told me to take him down the coast. I was not happy about the interruption or about being hijacked. I tried to get the gun then but we were interrupted by your friend."

"It doesn't make sense." He watched with concern as they carried Gage from the boat on a stretcher. "Are you hurt?"

"No, he got a gun butt to my temple right before Gage interrupted us. But I'm fine."

"You're coming to the hospital with me. You can be checked out while I'm tending to my sister. I have more questions for you."

BJ didn't fight it. He'd learned the best way to handle situations like this was to cooperate. Besides that, he couldn't shake the fact that he wanted to know how Gage came out.

And what had been so important that Gage would

risk being late to his wedding? It didn't make sense.

Especially when that groom had known he was running late.

CHAPTER FOUR

Shar was waiting when they wheeled Gage through the emergency doors at the hospital. She rushed to the gurney and covered his hand with hers as she hurried with them down the hall.

He was pale, so pale. His eyes were closed. IVs were hooked up to him and he had an oxygen tube at his nose. Tears formed in Shar's eyes but she didn't have time to cry. She could tell that Gage was not in a good way. "Gage," she said past the knot of tears. "Gage, you hold on. Do not leave me. Can you hear me? Fight, baby, fight."

To her surprise, his hand tightened in hers and though he didn't open his eyes, she saw him nod. Tears rolled down her cheeks and fell on their hands. And then his eyes opened and locked onto hers for one brief moment and Shar saw her life flash before her eyes.

"Fight," she urged, and then brushed her lips to his. She prayed that with this kiss she could show her love and she prayed this wasn't the last kiss they shared. "I love you, Gage Lancaster. And you will marry me."

His hand squeezed hers and then went limp.

A nurse gently pulled her away. "You can't go with him," she said. "Let them do their job."

"I love you," Shar called again as she relinquished her hold on his hand. And as he disappeared into the room, they closed the door and her heart went with him.

Shar was still standing there when her dad put his arm around her. "Come on, sweetheart. You come sit down before you fall down."

Shar couldn't move. She stared at the door and felt powerless. But her father's firm arm tightened around her.

"Come now, over here." He urged her to a seat where she could still see the door. Everything in the room seemed muted, as if she were sitting alone at the end of a tunnel.

Cam came and knelt in front of her. "How are you holding up? Was he able to speak to you before they got him back there?"

"He squeezed my hand. But he opened his eyes." She forced a small smile. "He's fighting."

"You fight too. Be strong, like you always are."

She stared at him. They all always told her how strong she was. Superwoman was her nickname. She felt weaker than a kitten right now.

"Shar." He shook her knees. "Focus. Do you hear what I'm telling you? He needs you strong."

She'd always been independent. Had always had an I-can-do-it-attitude. Had always felt she didn't need a partner in life as long as she had her family and her friends…and she knew in her heart of hearts that she could make it through whatever life threw at her. But Gage had come into her life and she wanted him now.

She didn't want to think about life without him. They were just getting started. Today was supposed to be the happiest day so far in her life. Instead, she was here in a waiting room and Gage was in the next room fighting for his life.

She sat a little straighter. "I'm okay, Cam. Just numb at the moment."

There was a commotion at the entrance and as if in slow motion, she looked that way and saw the rest of her family hurrying inside. She looked from them to Cam and her dad.

"I can do this." Her voice was stronger. "He needs me strong. He's going to pull through."

Her dad squeezed her shoulder. "That's our Superwoman."

And there was the nickname her family called her. It came in part from when she'd been small, she'd put on a cape and jumped from a tree to fly. She'd broken her arm and learned flying was overrated. But it was used now because she was dedicated to rescuing endangered and hurt sea turtles. She and Gage had met saving a loggerhead sea turtle.

Cam patted her knee. “This is the girl I figure he fell in love with. Though I barely met him, I figure any man who can have you falling in love with him must be some kind of man.”

She smiled through still damp eyes. “He is. You’ll love him.”

Before Cam answered, she saw Levi and a man she didn’t recognize walk into the hospital. The man waited by the door and Levi came toward her as the entire family did. They’d been gathered together, talking among themselves—probably giving Cam and her dad time alone with her. Levi stopped and spoke to a nurse and then came to her.

She stood as he reached her. As chief of police, maybe he could get her on the other side of that door. “Can you get me in the room with Gage?”

He gave her a hug and a tight squeeze. “No can do, baby sister. They work best without family in their way. I will do what I can to get you updates.”

“Thank you.”

“Shar, I’ve brought the man with me who was with Gage when he was shot by the convenience store robber."

Her gaze went to the man standing almost at attention beside the door. He was turned and looking out the door. "Who is he?"

The nurse went to the man and took him into an exam room. They left the door open but Shar couldn't see him now.

"He doesn't want to intrude but I had to ask him questions so I had him ride with me. And Shar, he and the gunman were struggling over a gun when Gage got on the boat and called out that he'd like to ask him some questions. He said the perpetrator told him to get rid of Gage and stood inside the cabin, hidden but with his gun on BJ—that's the man's name. He was basically rude and ended up demanding Gage leave the boat and go get married." Levi paused, his gaze narrowed. "He said Gage wouldn't leave. That he continued to say he needed to ask him some questions and then BJ thinks he realized someone was hidden and Gage moved toward the danger rather than run. BJ said it was odd. That he tried to get rid of him but the gunman moved into the line of sight and shot a bullet into the dock to warn Gage off. That shot is what was called in. It wasn't the shot that was fired when Gage dove for the gunman that hit him."

Shar's breathing slowed. "I don't understand. What was Gage thinking? Why did he stop?"

"I have no idea. What could be so important that Gage stopped by to see a stranger on a boat when he was running late to his wedding?"

Shar straightened, her heart stalled. "*Brandon,*" she thought and then realized she'd whispered it. "I…I need to see him." She started toward the room.

Cali took her arm. "Wait, Shar. If this is Brandon, maybe you should let Gage tell him. Maybe you should wait until you know. Until you have proof."

Jillian and her mother agreed.

"I need to see him. He was the last one to talk to Gage." *He was the last person who spent the last moments with him before Gage was shot.* "Why was Gage on his boat? Why did he stop there before the wedding? Had he had car trouble? Why? I need to know." She continued toward the room where the nurse had taken the man.

Levi fell into step beside her. "Okay. But I can tell you he doesn't know any of those answers."

Her brothers parted to let her by.

"We're here for you, sis." Jake gave her a killer smile of encouragement. "Gage is going to pull through. Remember, I saw him kissing you—he's gonna want more of that."

Max elbowed him and scowled. "Cut it out, Jake. She doesn't need you teasing her at a time like this."

Shar looked from Max to Jake, her adopted brothers who she loved as if they had her same blood. She thought of Gage and the bond he would feel for his half-brother when he found him. It would be a bond just as strong as hers to Max and Jake. "It's okay. I love all of you too."

"Me too," Trent added. "We're all here for you."

"I know." She paused, and looked around the room at the large family she was so blessed to have. "I know Gage. And there is only one thing that would have been powerful enough to make him late for our wedding. His missing brother. He's never had what we have. If he got word that this was his brother, then I feel like the pull and the need to find Brandon would have been too strong to let him pass right by and not stop."

Levi's brow etched into his forehead as it so often did when he was thinking hard. "But Shar, that's BJ McCall sitting in that room. And we've been looking for Brandon Jackson for the last month."

That had her hesitating. Then, without answering, she pushed past everyone and entered the room. The nurse had a blood pressure cuff on his arm but BJ McCall turned his head to look at Shar the moment she entered.

His gaze met hers and she gasped…the floor shifted as she found herself looking into the same eyes as Gage's beautiful teal-blue gaze.

"Brandon," she gasped. And then the world went dark.

CHAPTER FIVE

BJ shot off the exam table just in time to catch the bride before she hit the ground. Levi reacted also and together they moved her to the exam table.

"What happened?" BJ demanded. "She looked at me and fainted."

Levi smoothed his sister's hair out of her face as the nurse moved in and took her pulse. A beautiful older woman moved into the room to stand beside Levi.

"What happened?"

"I think she fainted, Mom." Levi looked over his shoulder at the crowd of people at the door. "The nurse will take care of her," he said, and they waited outside, giving the nurse room as she took the bride's pulse.

BJ stepped back too, giving the nurse and Levi and the mother room. He had seen the odd expression that had flashed in the bride's green eyes the moment his met hers.

Something was going on here and all he could do was wait until whatever it was came out. Her eyes fluttered open and she searched the room until she found him.

He wanted to know what was going on. *Why was she looking at him like that?* He didn't ask though, not now. She had enough on her plate with worrying about Gage.

She struggled to sit up. "I'm sorry. I never faint. But—" A doctor stepped into the room and Shar swung her legs over the edge of the exam table.

"Hold on." Levi grabbed her arm and held her still.

"How is he?" She looked as if she was ready to run to the room where Gage lay.

"He's been taken to surgery. They won't know the extent of the damage the bullet caused until the surgery.

Dr. Laura Burrows will be operating. She'll give you updates upstairs in the surgery waiting room. Nurse, can you show them where they can wait?"

"Yes, doctor," the nurse said.

"Is she okay?" The doctor looked at Shar with concern.

"She fainted earlier. But her pressure is normal now."

He nodded. "Understandable. But call me if you need anything." He patted Shar's hand. "Have faith."

"I do." Shar looked at the nurse. "Can you show me where I need to wait?"

BJ watched Shar's expressive eyes flash with what he could only classify as determination. She pushed her shoulders back and with her spine ramrod straight, she followed the nurse down the hall.

He followed them out into the hall and then stood outside the exam room and watched her go. Watched her family join her. He'd realized that the room full of men and women were her brothers and sisters. She had a huge family giving her support. He had one sister, Lilly, and suddenly he missed her.

Both of them had wanderlust in their blood. He for the sea and she for anywhere but the sea. Last time they'd talked, she was working at Yosemite National Park. But it had been a month since they'd talked and by now she might have packed her backpack and headed to the Grand Canyon. He thought that was on her list of stops but he couldn't keep up. He and Lilly had been on their own for much of their life after their parents were killed when he was nearly eighteen and Lilly had just turned seventeen. His mother had married Lilly's dad when BJ had been about four. His father was dead and Lilly's mother was dead and so their parents had made them all a family. While it had lasted it had been good. It just hadn't lasted…his parents had died far too young.

He needed to call her. It had been too long.

"Br—I mean, BJ." Shar had turned and was staring at him from down the hall. "Would you come with us?"

Levi turned to him. "If you don't mind, I can ask you more questions upstairs. I never finished."

BJ wasn't sure how many more questions the police chief was going to ask him but he still couldn't get the groom off his mind. He wanted to learn why the man had come on his boat and why Shar had fainted when she'd seen him. Because that was what it had felt like…their eyes had met and she'd passed smooth out. It had been seeing him, not worrying about her fiancé that caused her to faint. He was certain of it.

Why?

"Sure," he said. This had been the oddest day he could remember and he would see it through.

Upstairs, Shar sat down in the waiting room. She clasped her hands tightly together in her lap and took a deep breath and exhaled slowly. *She would get through this. She would not fall apart; Gage would need her.* When she got to see him after surgery, she wouldn't want him to see her tear-streaked face. She had to be strong.

Despite the pep talk she was giving herself, her lip began to tremble and she bit it hard trying to stop it. She focused on the good times they'd shared. He would make it through; she wasn't going to let herself think any other way.

She watched as Brandon moved into the room and stood just inside the door. He probably felt out of place. He was a great-looking man but the only thing about him that looked like Gage was his incredible eyes. As she studied him, he shifted his gaze and met hers. She looked away, wondering how she should tell him. Or whether she should tell him at all.

Cali came to sit beside her. "We're all worried about you but don't want to overwhelm you. There are a lot of us." She smiled and patted her knee. "I'm going to go get you something to drink. How would a cup of warm tea be? Or a cup of coffee? Or a water?"

"I don't need anything." Shar shook her head.

"But you do." Jillian sat on the other side of her. "How about warm tea with some honey for energy? You'll need your energy."

"Okay, then tea would be nice." It did sound good. And she understood her sisters' need to do something for her. She would be doing the same thing if it was one of them in this spot.

Cali hugged her. "He's going to be okay, Shar. We

are going to believe that."

"Yes." Jillian reinforced Cali's words.

Everyone needed to reassure her and she got that too. "Thank you both."

As her sisters left in search of warm tea, the seat beside her was taken by one brother after the other. She loved her brothers. There hadn't always been unity growing up but there had always been love. Teenage years for nine kids couldn't help but have some strain and yet they'd all made it and had a strong bond.

Gage had none of that. And now, he'd found his brother and he had to survive so that he could form a bond with Brandon.

Levi was talking to Brandon now and she rubbed her temple as again she wondered what to say to him. She'd asked him to come to the waiting room because she hoped that somehow, Gage would know his brother was near. And also so she could figure out what her next step should be. She stood and forced her weak knees to carry her across the room to Brandon and Levi. They stopped talking and she saw questions in Brandon's eyes.

"Can I have a few words with you?" Her heart fluttered as she stared into eyes so much like Gage's eyes. *Eyes that reminded her of what she would lose if Gage didn't make it through surgery.* She pushed that thought away. She would pray and believe and that was that.

"Shar, maybe you should wai—" Levi started to say, but she cut him off.

"It's okay, Levi. I won't keep him long. He was just the last person who was with Gage. I want to know about those moments before the shooting. I need to move around a little bit. Would you walk with me?"

He stared at her with kindness despite the fact that he must be overwhelmingly curious about what was going on.

"Sure," he said. "I'd be happy to walk with you."

Shar began walking and he fell into step beside her. *This was Gage's brother...and that meant, though Brandon or BJ didn't realize it, he was part of Gage.* And that comforted Shar.

Cali stopped beside Grant; he smiled gently at her and pulled her into his arms. “Is she doing okay? Anything we can do?”

“She’s holding her own.” She laid her head on his shoulder and breathed in the scent of him and the blessing of being in his arms. “I love you, Grant.”

He kissed the top of her head. “And I love you. I needed to hold you for a minute.”

She hugged him and then kissed his jaw. “I needed it too. We’re going to go to the cafeteria and grab her a cup of warm tea and honey. And one for ourselves too. Waiting is nerve-racking. Can we get any of you fellas anything?” She looked from her husband to her brothers, who had conveniently ignored her and Grant’s show of affection. Normally they might have teased them about it but not today.

Trent, who was standing closest to Grant and who had given Jillian a hug, smiled. “We can take care of ourselves. You two girls take care of Shar.”

Jake, Max, and Cam agreed.

“So there you have it,” Grant said. “Do y’all need help?”

"We've got it." She gave a smile. "We'll be right back. If that doctor comes out before we get back, call me immediately."

"Sure thing."

"Thank you," Jillian said. "We won't be long."

They hurried toward the elevator and pushed the button to the cafeteria floor.

"She's holding up," Cali said. "But I knew she would."

"Always," Jillian commented. "I wonder what BJ will think when they tell him their suspicions."

"I don't know. Can you imagine finding out you not only have a brother but also that you are inheriting half of a multi-million dollar corporation?"

"Talk about culture shock." Jillian gave a dry laugh. "But then, you just married a man worth more than I can count."

Grant just happened to be a world-famous sea life mural painter. Cali shot Jillian a sardonic look. "Hasn't changed me a bit, I hope."

"Of course it didn't," Jillian said. "Stuff like that doesn't impress you."

"Exactly. So maybe it won't matter to Brandon, or BJ."

They reached the cafeteria and within moments had their tea. There were tables in the area and Jillian walked to the table closest to the condiments. Cali followed her and saw there was a discarded newspaper on the table and a couple of gossip magazines. Jillian had set her two cups on the magazine and then turned to grab the honey. Cali was also carrying two cups, because they'd decided to grab one for their mom. She set hers on the table next to Jillian's and accepted the packets of honey her sister handed her. They both ripped open packets when Cali looked down at the magazine.

She stopped squeezing the sticky sweet contents into the paper cup of tea, her gaze caught on the photo beneath the paper cups. "What?"

Her brows knit together and she looked closer; pulling the cup off the page, she gaped.

Jillian gasped beside her. "*Olivia.* That's Olivia."

Cali moved the other cup and picked up the gossip paper…and both of them gaped at their sister. The third triplet.

She was locked in a passionate kiss with the mega-movie star Brad Pearson.

"This can't be right," Cali whispered. Olivia hadn't come home for months. She'd even missed Cali's wedding and hadn't made it up this weekend for Shar's wedding. She hadn't even called much.

"She's his publicist," Jillian said. "She knows better than to do this."

Cali looked at Jillian. "I don't know what's going on here but now's not the time to worry about it."

"I totally agree. Here, let me have that." Jillian took the magazine, rolled it up and then stuffed it into the big purse she carried. "There. We'll read it later and hope Mom or Dad don't see it. Right now we need to focus on Gage."

Cali took a deep breath and started squeezing honey into the tea and stirring furiously. "This has been a crazy day. First the wedding falling apart, then Gage being shot, his missing brother possibly being found, and now our level-headed sister, who knows not to get involved with a client, is on the front cover of a gossip rag."

"All true." Jillian sounded dazed. "I just can't

figure it all out. I hope the next thing that happens is that the doctor comes and tells us Gage is going to make it."

Cali picked up the cups. "I agree. I just hope no one else sees one of these magazines until Gage is okay."

CHAPTER SIX

BJ walked with Shar down the hall. Shar was holding up miraculously well, but he could see in her eyes and the waver of her lips sometimes that the effort was costing her. She was a strong woman. That much was evident.

Then why had she taken her first look at him and fainted?

And why did she look haunted every time their eyes met?

"Thank you for coming to wait with us. I'm sure Gage will want to talk to you when he wakes up."

"Why is that?" he asked. "I still don't know what he wanted from me when he stopped by my boat."

She looked thoughtful; her brow knit together and he could see her mind working behind those green eyes of hers.

"I really think that is for Gage to tell you. And I have my suspicions as to why he stopped by your boat but I don't know for sure. If I had his phone to check his messages, I might be sure what his reasons were."

"He had his phone in his hand before he was shot. It's probably on my boat somewhere."

Her expression brightened. "Then we'll tell Levi and he can have one of his officers bring it over."

BJ rubbed the back of his neck. It was knotted with tension. "I hope you don't take this wrong—I wouldn't want to upset you at all right now with what you have going on. But, this is all very strange. Stopping by my boat, me a complete stranger, putting himself in danger of being late for his wedding. Why would he do that?"

She stopped walking. "BJ, like I said, I have my suspicions but I can't reveal that to you. It's not my place. I can assure you that Gage will be able to explain it when he wakes up after surgery." She looked away as tears formed in her eyes.

He waited for her to blink them away and compose herself again.

"What does BJ stand for?" she asked.

"Brandon James."

"Oh, and do you have family around here?"

"No. From what my mother once said, we lived here when I was a boy, before my father died. So I finally decided to come take a look at it. I liked it and so I've been doing some charters and thinking about staying on for a little while."

Was he imagining that he saw her eyes flare with excitement?

He started to ask her again what was going on but someone called her name.

"Shar," her brother Levi called from behind her. "The doctor just came out."

BJ stored the questions for later. Right now he just hoped the doctor had good news.

Shar's heart lodged in her throat as she lifted her skirts and hurried down the hall toward the doctor. She came to a stop beside her father, and the rest of the family parted to let her stand in front of the pretty female physician.

All the emotion she was trying to suppress had been building to an overwhelming storm inside her with each passing moment that she hadn't heard about Gage's progress.

"How is he?" She nearly gasped, her words cracking.

"He's out of danger. The damage wasn't as extensive as it could have been, which is what saved his life."

Shar covered her face with her hands; she bit back a cry and fought the urge to fall apart. She grabbed her dad's arm. "He's going to be okay." She had once believed she didn't want to share her life with anyone. That a man would try to hold her back and curb her need to devote much of her life to the rescue of sea turtles and protecting the eggs on the beaches. But then Gage came along and turned her world and her thinking upside down. And now becoming Mrs. Lancaster was her heart's desire. To share her life with him as they both worked with the turtles.

But now all she wanted was him.

The doctor explained some details that she tried to keep up with but she just needed to know when she could see Gage.

"We'll get him in ICU and the nurse will come get you. I'll be checking on him periodically."

"Thank you," her dad told the doctor.

All Shar could do was nod. All she could think about was that she would see Gage soon.

Gage slowly began to come awake. He remembered much of what had happened. He remembered seeing his brother, the gun, and fighting for his life. He remembered Shar's kiss.

He'd taken that memory with him as he'd faded in and out in the emergency room.

"Gage. Can you hear me? I love you. The doctor says you're going to make it."

His heart thundered and he struggled to open his eyes. *He needed to see her. Needed to apologize for messing up the wedding.* And then he felt her press her lips to his.

Warm, sweet lips covered his and made him dizzy with love and longing for her. And he opened his eyes…her kiss showed him the way home.

"I want to wake up to those lips every morning," he murmured and wrapped the arm without the IV in it around her shoulders and held her tightly.

She cried then. Buried her face in his neck and sobbed. "Oh Gage. You came back to me."

He rubbed her hair, breathed in the soft scent of her and gently kissed her temple. "Of course I did."

She hiccupped and then took his face in her hands and kissed him. And then she looked at him so tenderly. "Did you stop to see your brother?"

His head cleared and he remembered. "Brandon. I'm sorry, Shar. I should have let it wait. But the information came through and I had to pass the marina on the way to the resort and I couldn't pass it by. I had to at least get a glimpse of him. I never meant to be late. To stand you up."

"I know. And I understand. But, he still doesn't know. I don't think he has realized that you and he share those amazing blue eyes with each other."

Gage managed a smile. "You noticed that?"

"Of course I did. And so has most of my family who knows what's going on. DNA will probably have to be done but the eyes made me a believer."

"They come from my dad." He remembered how sure he'd been the moment he saw BJ's eyes.

Shar caressed his face from temple to jaw. "He doesn't know yet. He's here and he has questions. But he has no idea about being your brother. Gage, he thinks his dad died when he was a small boy."

Gage closed his eyes, letting the information sink in. "It makes sense. From what we can figure, she married quickly, changed her name and may have been using an alias when she married."

Shar looked worried. "Don't stress too much over it right now. He's here. You'll have time to talk to him but right now you just need to get better. When you're out of the ICU, then you can think about this."

Gage rubbed her back. “You are amazing,” he murmured. “I love you. And right now all I want to think about is getting out of this bed and making you my wife.”

She smiled. “Soon. Rest now. I’ll be here when you wake up.”

His eyes drifted closed and he knew he had a smile on his face as the meds he was on pulled him back to sleep.

CHAPTER SEVEN

Two days after the shooting on his boat, BJ went back to the hospital. Shar Sinclair had called him and told him Gage would like to speak to him if he would come. "What time?" had been his only question.

He'd been busy over the couple of days since the shooting as he cleaned up his boat and waited. He'd mulled over everything that had happened and no answers to the mystery of what Gage Lancaster wanted with him had come. He'd researched Gage online. Learned from pulling up the wedding announcement that Gage was actually Benjamin Gage Lancaster, the son of Milton Lancaster, head of Lancaster Industries. He and his father had built Lancaster Industries into a hugely successful company.

He'd also learned that Gage was the heir of the company and since Milton's death, there was a lot of speculation about the company right now.

What did Gage Lancaster want with him?

And how could it have been so important that he had been willing to be late for his wedding?

Today he would find out.

He wore jeans and a blue t-shirt as he knocked on the door of the hospital room. Shar answered the door. She looked better without the worry and stress that she'd been riddled with two days ago. Her smile lit up her face as she greeted him.

"BJ, come in. Please."

Gage was sitting up in bed and he smiled when BJ walked in and held out his hand.

"You look better today. I'm glad you're okay."

Gage gave him a firm handshake. "Thanks. I'm supposed to be released tomorrow. And I thought about waiting until then to speak to you. But I decided this couldn't wait any longer. And you deserved to know what was going on."

"I have to admit that I'm curious," BJ said. "What would Benjamin Lancaster want with me?"

Gage looked at Shar; she went to stand beside him and from the drawer beside the hospital bed, she pulled out a yellow folder. She handed it to Gage and then placed her hand on his shoulder and smiled at BJ.

This was getting deeper by the minute, BJ decided.

"Shar told me that your father died when you were young. I'd like you to look at these photos."

BJ took the file and flipped it open. He was just ready to get this over with and get back to his life. He stalled, though, when he saw a picture of his mother and a man who was carrying a toddler on his shoulders as they walked down the beach. They were all smiling. Happy.

There were more photos of his mother and the older man, some with the toddler.

"Is that your mother?" Gage asked.

BJ met Gage's serious blue gaze and like that first time he'd met Gage, something felt familiar. "It is. But

I don't recognize the man." He looked closer at the toddler and it struck him that it was him as a baby. "And this is me? Right?"

Gage nodded. "It is. And that's my father, Milton Lancaster, holding you."

BJ studied the photos again. His mother looked incredibly happy. But she'd always looked happy. She'd been a loving woman with a big heart.

"We've been looking for you for years, BJ. We'd need to do a DNA test to be certain but I'm convinced you are my brother."

BJ's head whipped up from studying the photos. "Excuse me?"

"Believe me," Gage said. "I felt the same shock when the lawyer at the reading of the will told me I had a long-lost brother. It is one heck of a revelation."

BJ took a step back. His heart rammed against his ribs and his hands were cold. "My father died when I was a baby."

"No, your father died three months ago in Manhattan."

"Maybe you need to sit down." Shar spoke for the

first time. "It's a lot to take in."

"I'm fine standing."

Shar handed Gage another folder; Gage pulled a photo from it and held it out to BJ. "Your name is Brandon. This is my dad when he was your age."

BJ reached for the photo and stared at the headshot of Milton Lancaster. He looked at Gage and then he looked at the mirror on the wall over the sink behind Shar. Gage's eyes had been familiar because they were his eyes. They were Milton's eyes.

His gut tightened; he felt ill and the room was suddenly hot. *Why? If this was true, why would his mother have lied to him?* He asked the same question to Gage.

"From what my dad's friend and lawyer revealed to me, my dad wanted to marry your mother. He loved you and her, and he wanted to bring you home where I was and make us a family. But your mother was a free spirit who had no desire to move to New York. I think she grew worried that my dad would try to take you from her if she wouldn't agree to marry him. And to be honest, she might have been right. My father was used to getting what he went after.

"But then you and she suddenly disappeared from Windswept Bay and despite the investigators he hired to locate you, he never could. His PI got a lead on you finally but my dad, our dad, had a massive heart attack before the lead could be followed. I learned about you at the reading of the will. You, of course, will have to be tested just for legalities' sake, but you are now a partner in Lancaster Industries."

BJ just stared at Gage and then Shar. *This was crazy talk.*

"What if I tell you that I'm quite happy and satisfied with my life just the way it is?"

"You're still my brother and you're still my partner. Nothing changes that. And I have to tell you, I'm eager to get to know you. I have no other family except Shar and my future in-laws."

"We know this is a lot to take in, Brandon." Shar looked sympathetically at him.

"I prefer BJ," he said and knew it was gruff. *Unreasonable. But this was a lot to take in.*

"BJ." Shar smiled and came to touch his arm. "We know this is all a shock. But, there will be time to work it all out. However, we are going through with our wedding tomorrow and we would love for you to be there. Gage would love for you to be there."

BJ rammed a hand through his hair and tried to take it all in. He was a guy who went where the whim took him. He had a boat that he moved from port to port and a way of life that suited him. He was not a guy who wore a suit. "I think I need some time to think about this." He pushed the folders toward Shar.

"Those are yours. We have copies."

"Take them and we'd love to have you at the wedding tomorrow at three. We're moving it up. I'm tired of waiting to marry the woman I stood up once." Gage smiled at Shar.

BJ could see the love between them. But he wasn't willing to accept all that they'd said. Not yet. "I wish you both well and a happy wedding. But right now, I need to think."

Turning, he walked out of the room, down the hall and onto the elevator.

But as much as he wanted to deny that his mother had lied to him, something in his gut and in his eyes told him he couldn't. *He had a brother.*

And now, what was he going to do about it?

CHAPTER EIGHT

"Tell me he's out there," Shar said as Jillian hustled into the dressing suite with a huge smile on her face.

"Yes, he's out there. He's been here for hours. I think he camped out in one of the rooms so he wouldn't have to drive."

Cali chuckled. "I heard rumors from our brothers that he might have slept in his tuxedo so he'd be ready."

Shar laughed. "You are so funny. I was just teasing. I have no doubt that he's out there. He's been sending me sweet text messages all morning."

He wasn't moving very fast right now, with the wound still fresh, but he wouldn't have it any other way; he wanted to get married. And even though he'd not had any confirmation from BJ that he would be at the wedding, he'd said that all of that would work itself out in time. But it was time for a wedding. Past time for them to wed.

And she agreed.

There was a knock on the door and Jillian answered it. Her dad smiled at her from the doorway. "It's time, Superwoman."

Shar chuckled and could feel it all the way to her toes. "Nope, today I'm just me."

Gracie smiled over Sam Sinclair's shoulder. "Okay, ladies, it's marching time."

"Then let's get this show on the sand," Cali said, her eyes twinkling.

She and Jillian led the way and Shar followed them. She slipped her arm through her dad's and then one by one, her sisters started to walk down the path. There was a small pang of regret that Olivia hadn't made it, even after the delay, but Jillian and Cali had finally shown her the gossip magazine with Olivia's photo splashed over the front of it. And later she'd spied it at the grocery store. Her level-headed sister had gotten herself into an interesting mess.

Cali had spoken with her. Olivia had assured her that she had things under control and all was not as the photos and write-up had made it seem. She was handling it.

Shar figured her sister could do worse—she was, after all, kissing the number-one hottest ticket in Hollywood. Having her photo splashed across a magazine cover was probably a small price to pay for a kiss like that.

Then again, the only kiss Shar was interested in was the one Gage would give her when the preacher said, "You may kiss the bride."

Today she was selfish. This was her and Gage's day. She'd worry about Olivia later.

As the music started and she and her dad walked down the path that led to Gage, she saw him and her heart soared with the sea gulls drifting on the clouds in the soft blue sky.

His gaze locked with hers, and butterflies danced inside her. She had to hold herself back and walk with her dad at the appointed pace. But it was the longest walk she'd ever made.

She thought of the first day she'd seen Gage, jogging out of the surf to help her rescue a sea turtle. Even in that moment she felt a connection and it was one that would last a lifetime.

He smiled as she took her place in front of him and they joined hands. The sea air surrounded them; the gentle surf serenaded them as the pastor began leading the ceremony. They only had eyes for each other. And when the pastor said, "You may kiss your bride," Shar's heart thundered and she could not stop the smile that exploded across her face. Gage hitched a brow, winked one of his beautiful sea-toned eyes at her and then he wrapped her in his arms. "I'd sweep you into my arms if it weren't for my wound," he said, and then he kissed her with all of his heart.

"I love you, Mrs. Lancaster," he said after a long moment.

"And I love you," Shar murmured, and then tugged

his head back to hers and continued the kiss. This kiss was going to go on forever.

This has been a short story that connects *Somewhere With You* to the next book in the *Windswept Bay* series. Don't miss *Forever and For Always* as BJ McCall seeks to navigate the new turn his life has taken and Olivia Sinclair returns home to cope with the turn her life has suddenly taken…you won't want to miss *Forever And For Always*.

Excerpt from

FOREVER AND FOR ALWAYS

Windswept Bay, Book Four

CHAPTER ONE

Olivia Sinclair rolled over in bed and tugged the pillow over her head as the cat wailed just outside her window. "Go away," she groaned. She needed sleep. Just a little sleep was all she was asking for.

The wail came again.

"Give me a break, kitty," she groaned. "Go away."

She'd left Hollywood hours before dawn two days ago and driven the two thousand, three hundred miles to Windswept Bay. She'd tried to sleep for short periods in a couple of small-town hotels, one in the Texas Panhandle and one in Mississippi, but she hadn't been able to get much sleep while her mind was overtaxed with the scandal that was going on in her life.

She'd had to wear a baseball cap and sunshades every time she stopped for gas. And when she went inside a store for a cup of coffee or a soda, she'd had to keep her head down and hope no one standing in line with her happened to look at the cover photos on the magazine racks beside the counter…her picture was plastered over several of the tabloids. Of course, in most of them, her face was partly hidden by mega movie star Brad Pearson's face as he startled her with a kiss that came out of nowhere.

What had he been thinking? What had he been doing?

She was still reeling from it and the complications his odd action had produced in her life. The scandal his kiss had started threatened to end her career. He was her client at the public relations firm she worked for and until that moment, their relationship had been strictly business, as required by her firm. And her own moral code where clients were concerned.

She didn't want to think about that right now.

She wanted to sleep.

Something she hadn't had for days as she had been trying to stop the runaway media blitz the kiss had started.

The worst of it was that she should have seen it coming. Should have seen some sign that his feelings for her had shifted…but she hadn't.

The wail came again. *Maybe something was wrong with the cat…* She groaned and pulled the pillow from her head; she couldn't ignore a cat in trouble. She sat up. "Okay, okay."

She glanced at the clock and felt like crying. It was only five thirty. Blurry-eyed and feeling as if she were moving through a tunnel of sleep deprivation, she padded barefoot through the house and out onto the deck, only to realize it was a misty morning.

The mist had rolled in since she'd arrived a whole

three hours ago. She glanced down the short path and out across the very wide expanse of white sand that separated the bungalow from the water. The mist was probably going to turn into rain by the looks of the stormy early morning sky.

The wail came again and she spun to glance toward the sound. A small yellow cat sat on the edge of the roof.

"How did you get up there?" Olivia glanced around for a limb of some kind that the cat might have used. She saw one; she could see how the cat could have dropped from the branch of the ten-foot-tall palm near the end of the house or maybe it climbed up the firebush shrub and dove for the roof. Either one would clearly cause a problem getting back down. With a moan, Olivia bit her bottom lip and rubbed her forehead as the thought of climbing up a ladder to rescue the cat sank in. Her chest tightened at the very idea. Heights were not her strong point. Frankly, they were her Achilles' heel, terrifying her in a really petrifying way.

The cat wailed again and tilted its head to look down at her. It looked pitiful.

"Oh, this is so not good." But clearly, getting the cat down was the only way to get back to sleep. *She could do this.* She could get the ladder, climb to the roof edge, and scoop the cat up and rescue it, and then she'd climb right back down. No looking down, no looking around. She'd be okay.

She hurried from the deck to the small shed hidden in the trees for the groundskeeper of the larger estate that this bungalow sat on. Her sister had a really sweet deal going that enabled her to live in the bungalow and house-watch the place during the year for the seasonal owners. They rarely visited, as was the same for most of the other homeowners on the exclusive, private beach.

When she opened the door, Olivia spotted the ladder leaning against the wall; she pulled it out and then dragged it across the sand. She carried it up onto the deck and propped it against the roof and then checked it for sturdiness. Her mouth was dry and her palms damp—she could blame it on the mist but she knew it was perspiration. Sweaty palms were not becoming but when it came to heights, she had them.

Her stomach churned as she placed her foot on the rung and realized that she wore her shorty pajamas. She paused. *Maybe she should change.* The wail of the cat nixed that idea. Besides, there was no one around and she would only be using it as an excuse to put off what she must do. Her churning stomach turned into rough seas as she forced one foot at a time onto a new, higher rung. The mist caused the metal to feel slick, which only added to her anxiety. With her eyes barely squinting—this was to prevent peripheral sight—she reached the roof edge.

The cat, however, had retreated farther down the roofline.

Olivia tried to call out to the cat but only squeaked instead. She cleared her throat and tried again and this time actual words came out. “Here kitty, kitty.”

The cat wailed.

Olivia felt the dread of moving up onto the roof

all the way through her like a case of the flu gone bad, bad, bad. Her heart palpitations were erratic as she moved her hands to the top of the ladder. Gritting her teeth, she moved up a rung and then placed her hands on the roof and her fingers felt sick…like weak knees.

Ever since she was a child, she'd had this "problem."

"Focus on the helpless cat," she muttered and squinted at the roofline through one eye. "Do not look down." She enunciated each word like a decree and slowly crawled from the ladder to the wet shingles. She slipped and her foot pushed against the ladder rung as she frantically grappled for something to hang onto. Thankfully, she didn't slip down the roof.

But the ladder crashed to the deck, making her jump.

And making the cat run. It dove to the palm branch and disappeared from sight.

Olivia gaped, mouth open at the spot where it disappeared. "Ahh, why you," she said shakily just as the mist turned to a drizzle. And her weary spirits plummeted.

"Thanks a lot," she muttered darkly and shot a glance heavenward. "It's been a great week."

Focusing on not looking down and not slipping, she managed to move from her knees to her rump. The rough grate of the shingles did not feel good through the thin material of her PJs. Eyeing the satellite dish sitting just out of reach, but too shaken to move, she pulled her knees up and clasped her arms around them. Trying not to hyperventilate and starting to wail herself, she rested her chin on her knees and focused on the water in the distance. If she stared at the water, she could pretend she was nine feet down on the deck.

All she had to do was not look down and she'd be okay.

The problem was, how would she get off the roof?

BJ McCall wasn't sure what was more unexpected as he halted his jog on the rain-drenched private beach and stared at the small bungalow across the sand: was it the thoroughly soaked female perched on the roof, or that she had pink flamingos plastered all over the scrap of soggy wet material that she wore?

What was she doing up there?

It had been a long week and he'd had several consecutive sleepless nights adjusting to the fact that almost everything he'd believed about his life had been a lie. This news he'd just learned this past week had him still reeling and trying to come to grips with it. But he wasn't sure that was possible. Thus, his early morning jog on the misty beach…the private beach where his new brother's home was located. The home he'd just learned was half his.

Being a man who had never wanted a home or believed in being tied down, he lived on his boat and went where the wind or his notions carried him. The news he was processing was both disturbing and disrupting to his world as he knew it. Or wanted it.

The woman on the roof wasn't moving.

Was she real? Or maybe a figment of his sleep-deprived mind?

He rubbed his eyes, almost believing the woman perched on the roof like a weather vane in the middle of the rainy morning really could be a figment of his weary and overtaxed brain.

But when he squinted through the increasing haze of raindrops, she was still there.

Yep, she was as real as could be.

Learning that he had an older brother and a father he'd never known who had died recently and left him, not only an older brother and half of a huge home on a private beach in picturesque Windswept Bay, but also half ownership of a multi-million dollar company based in New York—*Manhattan*, New York—was a shock.

Manhattan. One place that, despite his wanderlust, had never appealed to him.

He wanted open space and the thought of all those buildings and sky only visible if you looked straight up was not on his bucket list.

And dollars… He was a simple man and had what he needed.

Need. This woman obviously needed help.

He moved forward and saw her tugging on the short gown, or maybe it was the top of a set of short pajamas. If she didn't look so miserable he might have smiled, but he felt bad for her and so there was no smile.

He strode toward the short trail to the house just as the drizzle suddenly turned into a downpour. And still she made no move to get off the roof. BJ frowned and started to jog. Something about this picture was definitely not right.

More Books by Debra Clopton

Windswept Bay Series

From This Moment On (Book 1)

Somewhere With You (Book 2)

With This Kiss (Book 3)

Forever and For Always (Book 4)

Holding Out For Love (Book 5)

With This Ring (Book 6)

With This Promise (Book 7)

With This Pledge (Book 8)

With This Wish (Book 9)

With This Forever (Book 10)

With This Vow (Book 11)

Check out Debra's Other Series

Cowboys of Dew Drop, Texas

Sunset Bay Romance

Texas Brides & Bachelors

New Horizon Ranch Series

Star Gazer Inn of Corpus Christi Bay

Cowboys of Ransom Creek

Texas Matchmaker Series

About the Author

Debra Clopton is a USA Today bestselling & International bestselling author who has sold over 3.5 million books. She has published over 81 books under her name and her pen name of Hope Moore.

Under both names she writes clean & wholesome and inspirational, small town romances, especially with cowboys but also loves to sweep readers away with romances set on beautiful beaches surrounded by topaz water and romantic sunsets.

Her books now sell worldwide and are regulars on the Bestseller list in the United States and around the world. Debra is a multiple award-winning author, but of all her awards, it is her reader's praise she values most. If she can make someone smile and forget their worries for a few hours (or days when binge reading one of her series) then she's done her job and her heart is happy. She really loves hearing she kept a reader from doing the dishes or sleeping!

A sixth-generation Texan, Debra lives on a ranch in Texas with her husband surrounded by cattle, deer, very busy squirrels and hole digging wild hogs. She enjoys traveling and spending time with her family.

Visit Debra's website and sign up for her newsletter for updates at: www.debraclopton.com

Check out her Facebook at: www.facebook.com/debra.clopton.5

Follow her on Instagram at: debraclopton_author

or contact her at debraclopton@ymail.com

www.ingramcontent.com/pod-product-compliance
Lightning Source LLC
Chambersburg PA
CBHW070506170726
48291CB00008B/2681